Mom
Can't See
Me

Sally Hobart Alexander

Photographs by George Ancona

Macmillan Publishing Company   New York

Collier Macmillan Publishers   London

For their help and cooperation in making this book possible, I
wish to thank Bob Alexander, Jay Budde, Camp Crestfield, Shannon
Daley, the East Hills Elementary School, the Frick International
Studies Academy, Steve Greenberg, Gymkhana, Hit or Miss, Marilyn
Hollinshead, Warren Hollinshead, Carol Knight, the Manor Movie
Theater, Richard Nicklos, Point Park College, Annie Puskar, Jean
Puskar, Norman Rabold, Andrew Tinker, Eben Waggoner, Karen
Waggoner, Charlotte Weber, and Jennifer Weinberg.

Text copyright © 1990 by Sally Hobart Alexander
Photographs copyright © 1990 by George Ancona

Macmillan Publishing Company
866 Third Avenue, New York, NY 10022
Collier Macmillan Canada, Inc.
First Edition. Printed in the United States of America.
10   9   8   7   6   5   4   3   2   1

The text of this book is set in 14 point ITC Cushing Book.
The illustrations are black-and-white photographs.
Design by George Ancona.

Library of Congress Cataloging-in-Publication Data
Alexander, Sally Hobart.   Mom can't see me / Sally Hobart Alexander:
photographs by George Ancona. — 1st ed.   p.   cm.
Summary: A nine-year-old girl describes how her mother leads an
active and rich life despite being blind.
ISBN 0-02-700401-5
1. Blindness — Juvenile literature. [1. Blind. 2. Physically handicapped.]
I. Ancona, George, ill.   II. Title.
RE91.A44   1990   617.7′12 — dc20   89-13241   CIP   AC

To Bob, Joel, and Leslie, with applause — S.H.A.

And this one is for Isabel — G.A.

N ine years ago, when I was born, Mom could pick me
out of a bunch of babies. I had the biggest feet.
Mom had to find me that way because she can't see.

When she was twenty-six, blood vessels inside
her eyes started breaking. The blood didn't show,
but soon it made her blind.

Some blind people can see colors or blurry
blotches, but my mom can't see any of those
things. She's totally blind and can't even tell if
a light is on or off. She doesn't see black, just
smoky white or gray. Once I put a scarf over my

eyes and tried out being blind. I got lots of bumps, just like Mom, so I took off the blindfold. Mom can't take off her blindness. She doesn't seem sad about it, just frustrated when she can't find things quickly.

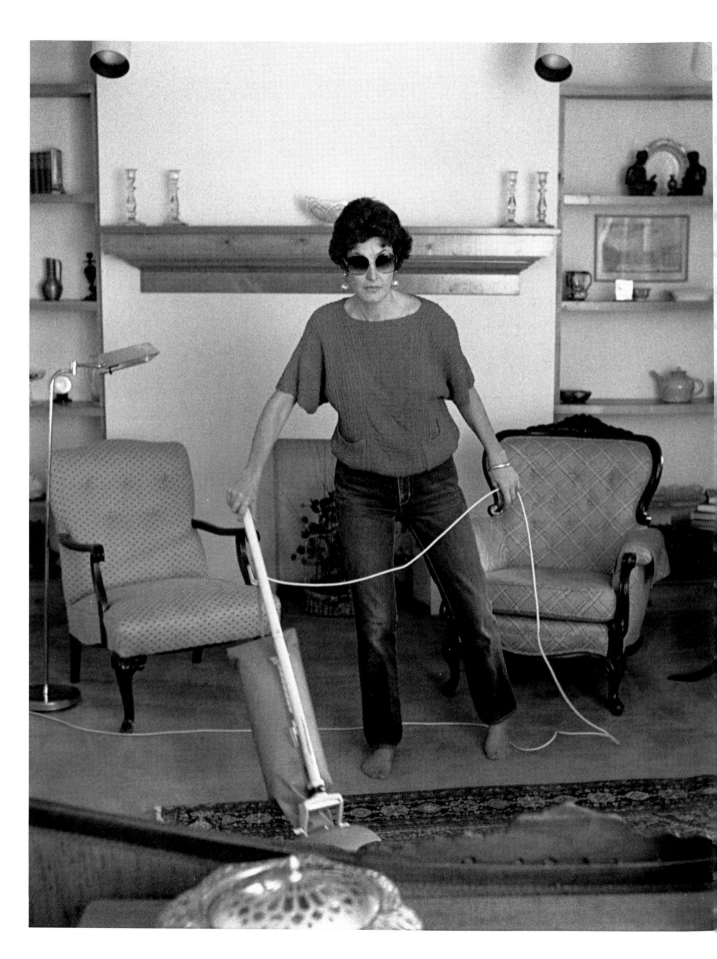

Except for her eyes, Mom looks completely normal. She wears sunglasses, even in the house. They make her prettier and safer from open cupboard doors and other things that could hit her.

When Dad first saw Mom in those glasses, he thought she looked like a movie star. Later he learned that she was funny and independent, too, and asked her to marry him. My big brother, Joel, makes a face when he hears this story, but I love it and tell everybody.

When I was four months old, Mom says I already understood that she was blind. At a "Mothers' Day Out" program, other babies smiled when their mothers came for them. When Mom came for me, I squeaked and gurgled and made all kinds of noises so she could find me. I still make noise for Mom, especially when Joel silently teases me. If I screech, Mom comes to the rescue.

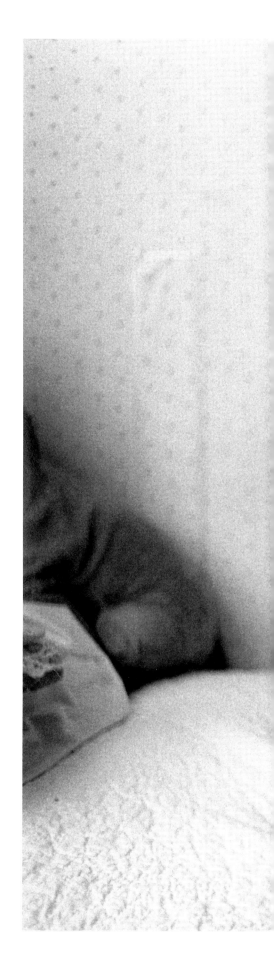

Not everybody understands about having a blind mom. I wish they did. My friends always nod or point when they talk. Since Mom can't see what they're doing, I have to explain. I feel like a translator.

Mom does some things differently, but mostly she's like other mothers. She walks with Marit, her guide dog. Marit leads Mom around telephone poles and anything else that might bump her.

I'm glad that Marit can go everywhere with us — on buses, to restaurants, to school, even in a canoe.

Joel and I play with Marit when she stops working. As soon as her harness is off, Marit drops her toy frog at our feet and barks till we play.

When I was little, Mom made *me* wear a kind of harness and leash, too, so she could feel where I was. After the first morning of nursery school, my new friend, Charlotte, asked her mother, "Why is the lady pulling Leslie on a rope?"

Mom used to put jingly bells on my shoes so she could hear me. When I wanted to stay longer at nursery school with Charlotte, I took off my shoes. Then Mom couldn't find me.

I still do things that Mom doesn't know about right away. If Dad's not home, I switch the light back on to read way after bedtime. Once I sneaked some cookies so quietly that Mom couldn't possibly have heard the lid clang. But then she asked, "Why are you eating chocolate chip cookies so close to dinner?" I forgot that she could smell them on my breath.

When we were younger, Mom read to Joel and me, but she had to use books with braille bumps, as well as print and pictures. Our favorite was *The Little Engine That Could.*

Braille is hard to learn. I tried it. Even when I remembered how many dots stood for a letter, I couldn't always feel each one. Mom's fingers weren't that speedy at reading it, so sometimes we said the printed words before Mom could read the braille ones: "I think I can. I think I can."

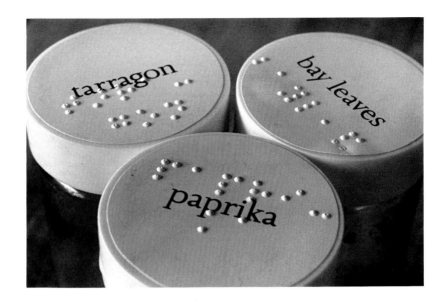

Mom uses braille recipes and braille labels when she cooks. For baking, we use a braille timer so that our cookies don't burn. "May I lick the bowl?" I always ask. "Of course, Leslie," Mom says. She doesn't know how much of the batter I've already eaten.

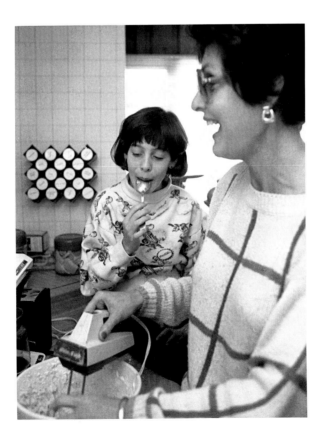

Most mothers drive, but not ours. She walks us places or takes us by bus. On long trips, to our piano lessons and back, for instance, she tells us parts of an exciting story like *Treasure Island*.

Mom can borrow huge books on cassette tapes from a library. Whenever Dad takes us out in the car, we play them. And on camping trips we all like to listen in our tent, even Marit.

Mom takes me to the movies. I tell her what's going on in the silent parts. If they're exciting, she has to remind me to whisper.

She takes me to musicals. *My Fair Lady* is the one we like best, and we know the words to all the songs. We sing them, very loudly, while Mom curls my hair.

Mom and I take tap dancing lessons together. At my cousin's wedding we tapped to the tune of "Tea for Two."

I also dance when Mom plays the piano. There's braille sheet music, but Mom plays by ear. Sometimes Mom and I play duets, the way she and her dad did years ago. I always open the front door so the people on my street can listen.

At my gymnastics class, Mom can't tell my thumps from anybody else's. I'm still glad she's there. Once a girl in my class asked Mom, "Can you see anything?" Her mother scolded her, but I said it was okay. Joel and I ask other handicapped people questions. We think it's being interested, not rude.

On Saturdays Joel and I ride our bikes. Mom and Dad come along on their two-seater. "Mom pedals, and I steer," Dad always says. The bike is so unusual that everybody stares at us, but they don't know that Mom is blind.

Mom plays baseball with Joel and me. Joel calls her the "designated hitter." She can't catch, but if she throws the ball up herself, she sure can hit.

She takes me swimming. We like the neighborhood pool best because the lanes are roped off and she can't crash into any other swimmers.

On Tuesdays Mom volunteers at my school. It makes me feel important. She talks about books in the reading classes. Sometimes kids tell her stories, which she types into books for them.

Before she became blind, Mom taught elementary school. Now she's a writer. She has a computer that speaks every word she types. When I interrupt her at the computer, she makes it say, "Give me a smooch, Leslie."

Until Mom got the computer, she used a regular typewriter. I read her chapters onto tape. Once Mom typed a story all over my math homework. Luckily my teacher could find my answers, and she read Mom's story to the class.

I guess Mom makes more mistakes than other mothers. But mostly they're silly ones, like spraying lemon furniture polish, instead of starch, when she was ironing my dress.

Mom made the funniest mistake at the airport. She threw her arms around a man who sounded like her brother. It was the pilot, but he laughed and hugged Mom back.

Sometimes her mistakes embarrass me, like when she keeps talking to a clerk who's walked away. I nudge her and say, "She's gone."

Or when Mom answers people who are not even talking to her. Once, in a hotel, a man said, "Oh, you're beautiful!" Mom thanked him, but he explained, "I was talking to your dog."

At Joel's soccer games, all she hears are twelve-year-olds puffing and thudding down the field. When the crowd cheers and I say, " Joel scored," she jumps up and screams, even if the rest of the people have gotten quiet again. This makes me cringe. But the worst was the time I goofed and told her Joel had scored when he hadn't. Mom jumped up and yelled, "Way to go, Joel!" Joel's face got all red, and he called right from the field, "Eben scored, Mom, not me!"

When I tell Mom I'm embarrassed, she pulls my nose and says, "That's what parents are for, embarrassing their kids!"

I think I'm a little different from kids with regular mothers. I don't always laugh at jokes that call somebody blind just for not seeing something. To me that's not exactly funny.

I have to remember things better. If I forget to pack my lunch or homework, Mom has to ride two buses to get to my school.

I help Mom more, reading to her and telling her if her lipstick is crooked. I also wash fingerprints from the walls and stains from my clothes. Mom pays me for being her special helper.

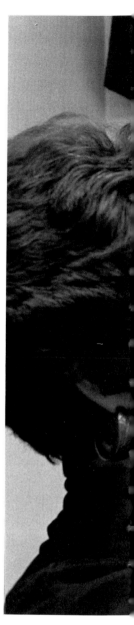

Charlotte thinks it's funny that Joel and I put Mom's
hand on things we describe to her, like a design I created
or a puppet Joel made.

I hold Mom's hand, sit on her lap, and hug her a lot. I
tell Charlotte it's the same as her smiling at her mom,
but I think it's better. Joel says he's too old for this mushy
stuff, but Mom hugs him, anyway. "Blind parents get
special privileges," she says. Mom plans to hug us till
we're forty-five.

"When I'm forty-five," I tell Joel, "I bet there'll be a way to fix Mom's eyes." He doubts it. But he wishes Mom could see him when he's swimming freestyle or zooming on his skateboard. I sure wish Mom could see, especially when there's something too wonderful to describe, like the Grand Canyon or Niagara Falls.

I wish she could see me, too. Mom says she'd love to get a little peek at me or Joel or Dad. Since she can't, she says she takes a double share of touching and hearing us. My aunt tells her I look just the way Mom did when she was a "nine-year-old squirt with a gap between her new teeth." So I guess Mom has a pretty good picture of me. Anyway, every time I have a birthday, I make two wishes over the candles — one for me and one for Mom.

I tell Joel I'm scared about becoming blind some day. He says you can't catch blindness like chicken pox. Besides, our doctor says we can't inherit Mom's kind of blindness.

Mom sure doesn't seem scared. Once she did something that none of my friends' mothers ever did. She climbed all across a rope course, high in the trees. I was really nervous watching her, but Marit was even worse. She barked the whole time. Afterward I was very proud. Mom was so brave.

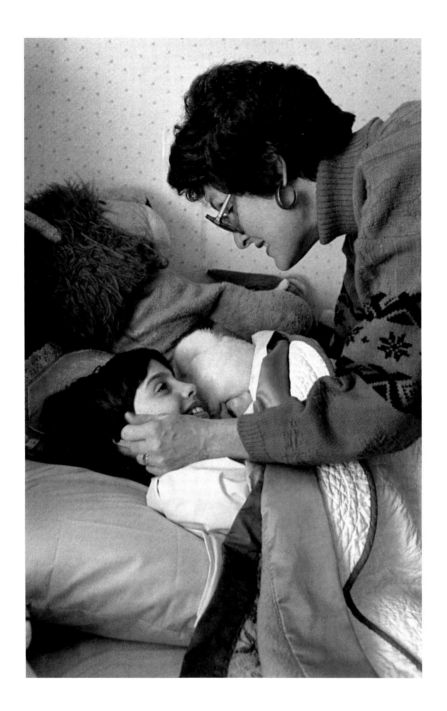

Mom sure is silly, the way she wakes me up for school in the morning and pretends to gobble me up or kiss me and tickle me all over.

She says she can *still* pick me out of a bunch of kids. I'm the skinniest girl on the block, and I still have the biggest feet.